Guided Instrument

P. Marquez-Garcia

AuthorHouse™
1663 Liberty Drive
Bloomington, IN 47403
www.authorhouse.com
Phone: 833-262-8899

Because of the dynamic nature of the Internet, any web addresses or links contained in this book may have changed since publication and may no longer be valid. The views expressed in this work are solely those of the author and do not necessarily reflect the views of the publisher, and the publisher hereby disclaims any responsibility for them.

This book is printed on acid-free paper.

ISBN: 978-1-6655-6991-0 (sc)
ISBN: 978-1-6655-6990-3 (e)

Library of Congress Control Number: 2022916304

Print information available on the last page.

Published by AuthorHouse 08/31/2022

authorHOUSE®

CONTENTS

DEDICATION

To my brother dan, my FATHER, my FAmily members and all those enriched military- social humanitarians whom unequivocally sacrifice in Everything, helping, inspiring, and standing strong to their true Noble beliefs that make a great impression on American society, and humanity.

God bless

ABOUT THE AUTHOR

Pablo Marquez-Garcia, grew up in various places around the world. As a child his activities included hiking, swimming, biking, football, baseball, basketball, reading and guitar playing. He attended Pedro A. Campos High School and is a graduate of Friends University.

Having a Human Resources Degree, he has worked primarily in the logistics field and has traveled extensively to various countries to implement Materials and Purchasing departments and speaks fluent Spanish and English along with conversational German.

Married to Iris and having three wonderful children, he emphasizes reading and creative thinking to them. He has authored several Novels among them Children's Novels as; <u>Benito's Treasure Hunt</u>, and <u>Flight To The Mountain Top</u>, written as a remembrance to his various childhood experiences while growing up and in sharing them with his children.

Recently, he has published two other Novels'; <u>Costume</u>, <u>Guided Instrument</u>, and <u>Cruise'In</u>, these directed to a more adult audience as he narrates how life's defunct characters can turn certain incidences into real life positive satisfaction with the help of friends.

ACKNOWLEDGEMENTS

Parents Pablo and Aida, Iris and kids, along with grade school
teachers - Mr. Schiovane, and Mr. Edwards

And

To those that created in me to seek goodness and love in my own lifetime.

Chapter 1

GROWING OLD

Excited and overwhelmed they entered the most rowdy Cafe in the City. Everyone was in their private party of audacious roar but lifting their smiling heads as the two graduates past them by. Congrats! One or another burst out in loud voice, as the aroma of rum, beer and schnapps made its presence overly prominent.

Over here! Samuel! Josh! They sooner synchronized and found their group through the misty low-lit tavern-like seats, where they'd spend the following hours celebrating. They hugged and mach valiantly acted out their ritual of four years of camaraderie they had developed throughout the years at Sacramento Prep College. A privy selected College on the out shirks of the great City.

Throughout the night they exchanged thoughts, jokes and reminisced of this day, that finally had arrived.

It was then that Josh told a story about Junior High School that was the routine way of showing their allegiance to each other and with that story Josh looked over to Samuel who by this time was the center of attraction and would now tell his tale about someone else that would be privy or perhaps not so privy after today. They recounted the many childish mischievous ways they would find humor in certain past daily activities and how now after today their lives would change with the advent of their careers and devotion to their calling, their new evolution into the workplace.

Continuing into the night that swept its way towards morning, their giddy selves and flagrant outbursts even found humor and delight in taunting ways and in telling tales. Their degree of patronage they had throughout these years to the old Armageddon they defined and soon forget, lead to songs of jubilee and college year fraternity chants.

For Samuel and Josh it was special since both had grown up in the same neighborhood for a maximal of time. Their childhood past riddled with sports, girlfriends, angry teachers, school elections and a complaint here or there were now imprinted into their psyche and no one was to change neither that nor their close friendship. Many people would envy the past years of having been on the same baseball team, the same soccer team and the accolade math-bee during their junior and high school years. They'd even shared the same kindergarten teacher, Ms. Juniper, which was still around the City, not teaching any longer but present and willing to make a comment or two when she would run into them throughout the years. And of the small stuff, they were really two gentlemen with the luxury to have been raised in a neighborhood where they knew each other, understood each other and respected each other, as friends, and now as graduates!

Josh Ashcrupt, was now the new graduate of Political Science with a Minor in Computer Science. He had always been able to excel in school and his parents expected no less small things from him than to be the best. Josh took this advantage and sought two degrees that would surely impress his parents, well - he thought. But in all regards he was equivalent to a Kissinger / Karpov in their fields and during their time.

Samuel Ponce, also graduated with a Computer Science Major and had become very instrumental to Josh when he was running from book to book and needed extra assistance to complete his programming class or D-Base special computer coding course. They both helped each other enormously and both had succeeded extremely well in their endeavors.

Josh for one was on his way to Washington, via Harvard for a few more classes that would enable him to start politics and law for the Senator he was to be coached by. Josh's parents ensured he'd be well versed for the day he'd take on the very important work they'd worked out years in advance with the Senator. There were no trials, misconceptions nor misjudgments, Josh was there committed and totally at the disposition of the Senator and his projects. This would make Josh's parents proud that they had accomplished this dream in a generation's time. To have a family member work for the highest office - Washington DC.

Samuel hired to assist in Princeton's new faculty building where they had been housing the newest Computer Statistical Laboratory in the United States. They both were very modest, proud and exceedingly anxious in starting their futures and used their gathering to bid each other good-bye - until they would meet again. Songs rang out as they'd shimmy out of the Cafe doors that night onto the streets on their way home.

Chapter 2

FRIENDSHIP DEFINES ITSELF

Couple of years had gone by; each meant a great step into the growth and prosperous futures these two young men had in store for each other. For Josh, he was now serious with a young oligarchy lady that had a direct tie to the Congress of the United States. He had decided that she was to be his future lady, but everyone knew with his outspoken manners that he meant, "this is my ticket to a sure future, Executive Branch or Legislative Branch". The young aspiring lady wasn't at all surprised by his pompous attitude and would only smile when this characterization would be forwarded.

Samuel on the other hand had launched his first Computer Model for Princeton and was now working with a very secluded, highly classified computer consulting company as the director for research in viruses, artificial intelligence security and firewalls.

Tonight they'd meet on Josh's grounds for one of their unique get together. Arriving by taxi at the address Josh had given him was exciting and surprising; he made himself into the gathering of political elites that night where he found Josh and his lady - to be.

"How's the war?" shouted Samuel out to Josh. Josh responding in their homegrown lingo, "we're there and the fires lit!" As they embraced the hug was that of old friends reuniting after several long years of not seeing each other, sounds of pats and grunts came from these two young men as if brotherhood was the co-signature of their lives. They were excited and thrilled of anticipation of having loads of things to talk about and how their professional life's were progressing. That night went fast as they all ended together, Samuel with his newly found girl, from the Armed Forces Department.

They talked about their own developments and the new ones that were to happen and when speaking about those things, secrecy things; they'd lean over their shoulders, as if to see - if anyone was close enough or listening in. This gave the gals the opportunity to smile and make suggestive signs that the night was over, but these two gentlemen weren't about to make it end. They talked and talked about the way things were, to what they were believed to have been, and to what it was like now. How the Political System was needing a revamp to keep up with the new changing times, to how computer programs in college were obsolete and how in a matter of such short times, newer and better software's were developed and being developed.

The sun dawning, the gals had no alternative but to pry them apart as they ran away from each other for the remaining of the morning night, which had already awaken.

After a few more days of seeing each other on the Capitol grounds and Samuel sightseeing around and getting to know better his newly found lady, he was back at Princeton, continuing his new Project.

Without regard, they'd see more of each other in the near future.

Chapter 3

FAMILY TIES

Samuel threw down the phone with outrage and disgust! "Dam It! Doesn't she know who I am?" He walked around the Computer Lab pacing like a wild tiger in its homemade cage. Impatient with bouts of anger, infuriated and disbelief. Samuel had just received a call by his Uncle, his Grandmother was dead. His Uncle said something about the Military Base buying up the land a year or so ago; and in practicing maneuvers fired a missile that ended in his grandmother's life while in her garden house where she'd spend at her late, fall of years, time making sure her rhododendrons and magnolias would make the transition from the many years they had grown them in their twenty-five acre property. "But why wasn't Josh calling me back?!" Samuel muttered to himself.

Samuel in dismay, cried like a baby while his tears were still molten-moist, he continued making calls to his needed partner, Josh. Within him he thought, Josh would be able to resolve his pain; he'd certainly help find out how this would have occurred to his Grandmother and specially; while she was still living there.

"Damn it!" As he heard the message machine click into message mode. It was late maybe he's gone for the day, he thought. The following day Samuel spoke to Josh which lead them to meet in Washington, where Samuel for sure would get a legitimate answer and maybe see some retribution for what had happen to his grandma. As always Samuel and Josh met and embraced, as Josh spoke solemnly about the tragedy and the loss of his family member.

Samuel sat slump and intoxicated from the couple of whisky-sours he'd had the previous nights and air flight, trying to surmise how this would have happen. Its' not that Samuels family had not been participatory in the rich history of country or that of the United States? His Grand Father had served with the Cavalry in the big one, which was what WWI had been remembered by, and his father also had served this country by going which today everyone knows it was an obligatory drafted. But regardless, they had served this country well. Why would the Military do this?

Josh was going about his daily calls and inquiries as best he could and tried to console his friend the best he could by sympathizing for him and letting him know he'd check into it.

You know Josh; my family has lived in that area for well over seventy-five years. Hell! I remember, seeing the first telephone poles go up in that neighborhood. My Grand parents made a great party for everyone celebrating that innovation to the area. Folks from across town came in their automobiles and celebrated the occasion by calling their families and happily letting them know they'd soon be getting own telephone too!

"I know Samuel", remarked Josh, as he silenced the voice on the other end of the telephone line to pause a moment.

We'd never go against imminent domain of the Government but why would they start maneuvers there and then be so reckless? Why did my Grand Ma die in such a travesty?!

Samuel was heartbroken and only knew he would have to leave and join his family for the funeral arrangements and all. This is going to be a hell of funeral specially, that we would have preferred to honor her for what she had done over this reckless behavior. And Josh, I have to tell you, I was told before this happen there was a problem several years ago when they started moving the bomb droppings closer to Grand Ma's home. The neighbors told them a long time ago when they were driven out of the area because of the noise and fear. "Why don't you drop one on your family's house" or "better why not drop one here, so that we can sue the pants off you!" They didn't take Government intervention too lightly back in those days and Grand Ma was a feisty old lady the few times I had seen her last.

This all happened while Samuel was well into his post-graduate years and no-one wanted to bother him with the details, but now let the truth be heard, Samuel's riveting memories flashed from one thought to another. They said good-bye and Samuel headed home from the funeral

Chapter 4

FOUL PLAY

By now Samuel was well into his career making advancements with computer technology and services that placed him in high recognition in the tech community and foremost in the programming community. His anger and memories of grand ma were missed and overcome by daily analytical work and daily stresses of life. But his thoughts and memory were those of grandma his friends and a cool pitcher of lemonade.

He had had several high presentations nation wide and several local and specialized articles written about his breakthroughs and new technological advances. At times Samuel thought of starting his private consulting firm to expand his career.

One day while surveying several offers he ran across an offer he thought to be a gracious and promising one. He thought he'd look into it and was surprised to find it led to an "initiative" Program sponsored by a Washington Office. As he made his preparation to find out more about the proposal and the application process, he sought out to find the sponsors for this opening. When he found the person, he was surprised it was his lady friend who had worked for the Armed Forces Services and had had several dates with her throughout the years. He called her and they conversed a little bit about the position and how it would develop and why this new position was of high interest for the Armed Forces Services.

A few hours into having spoken to her, Samuel received a call from Josh. Hi, "Samuel how's it going? How's life treating you?" Josh commented in a pompous manner. Samuel was surprised by the call and thought what a coincidence his friend would be calling, after all, he was just talking to someone in his area and he'd surely want to know when they'd be together again, like," two peas in a pod".

"Josh, by the way, I just spoke to the Armed forces Services for a position in a new developing program? We might see each other soon?" answered Samuel.

Josh was not to aroused and told Samuel, "you'd better think about it, you know these are sometimes just for several years, and then they close up operations".

Samuel was surprised, "Well; I'm glad I asked about it, because you know more than anyone else does". With that Josh hung-up the telephone as Samuel's thoughts of being close to his friend were in a way snuffed out but lead him to believe it was the daily grind that made the conversation short.

The following week he was surprised to hear from his lady friend at the Armed Forces Offices that were hiring for this prestigious position.

"Samuel, we're still waiting for your information, you have the job!" She spoke enthusiastically. "Why haven't you gotten that stuff over to me, dream cakes?" She said as she giggled.

"Well, I thought about calling you but I spoke to Josh and he wasn't too sympathetic with the duration of the Program and I thought why start if it will only end shortly thereafter?" Samuel responded.

"Josh doesn't know, why would he say that?" She inquired surprised. I'll put you in for an interview next week, I'm sure you're the candidate they need and want, and with those words she hung-up.

Samuel was perplexed and decided maybe Josh was playing with me or maybe he's not aware of the particulars. Samuel decided to review the possibilities again and promised himself he'd find out why the distance.

After several intentions to make his inquires known by phone, and computer e-mail; he was not progressing through the Washington Department's computer Web-site. He tried several avenues and left several inquiries to which he received no responses back from the technical e-mail inquiry department of the Armed Forces Services Web-site. He knew that they had prepared well their programming to avoid un-wanted access to several areas they deemed, "secret" or "top secret". But without any fear that this was what he wanted in his life he proceeded to the interview set-up by his girl friend.

As he arrived he was greeted and sat in front of several people that had to approve of his appointment and was asked several questions relating to computer programming, firewalls, developments and his views. Samuel was impressed not by the questioning but the atmosphere of elite-ness, and reverence of superiority these individuals had to each other, it made him feel that this was an appointment that would merit his true loyalty of community and country.

Within several hours they all adjourned the meeting with high spirits, when Samuel and his lady friend reached the door there stood Josh.

"Hi! Samuel. How'd it go? Do you think you got the job?" He smirked as he smiled at his lady friend in a cavalier way. "Well, I'm sure hoping so. I didn't expect you'd be here? What has brought you here, Josh?" asked Samuel.

"Well, I guess its time you should know for whom you'd be working for?" Josh announced as he paraded to an executive chair within the room.

"Samuel, you know I wouldn't do anything to hurt you? Right? But you've practically forced me to tell you this now and in front of your friend."

"What is it? What could it possibly be?" Samuel you are very intelligent but this position requires more than knowledge! We need someone with "balls"! This career takes many years of training, molding and subjugation. It took me many years to accept this calling and I'm the best!

"What do you mean, Josh? I like competition and being motivated by others?" responded Samuel.

You don't get it do you Samuel? You're just like the rest of the herd, you follow! You don't understand the dynamics of this business and you'll never learn! It takes more than just wanting to have the United States ahead of everyone; you have to make it ahead of everyone! Spewing his words in an intense manner, Samuel and his lady friend were baffled by his outburst.

"Josh, clam down this isn't dentistry we're practicing here!" answered respectfully Samuel.

But Josh just inhaled to calm himself, and bolted out the doors without a farewell nor a friendly good-bye, pure apathy.

Samuel and his lady friend sat in the room for several minutes, motionless to what they had just witnessed. Samuel finally got up to leave, headed for the double mahogany doors. As he was almost through, she pulled on his briefcase. Samuel, don't leave me this way, please! Samuel turned to hear and in a sub-toned voice said," It's over, I know when I'm not wanted ", and he followed through the doors and let them close before her without looking back.

Samuel's thoughts were ricocheting back and forth on his way back home. Thoughts of finding out why his best friend acted like this and what were his motives. He obviously was naive to something more than what he could imagine.

Chapter 5

LOOK IN THE MIRROR

Samuel headed out to his normal workload as he had for the past ten years not in doubt that his contribution was going to matter today. His newly formed Agency was going to lead him to the integration of the best firms ever to exist with the capabilities of updating and launching programs simultaneously not seen in any public or private company today. He was proud of his accomplishments and was very grateful to those that had stuck with him throughout his whole tenure in Princeton.

As he arrived at work they greeted him with a celebration and a check for his next development of his program which Samuel was going to put down as a payment on a new downtown office where he'd be working out of shortly. Everyone was enjoying the party atmosphere when he was told a call from Washington was on hold for him. When he picked it up in his office phone it was an unknown person, "don't go home today" the voice said and hung-up. Samuel asked if anyone knew the caller but the celebration was in full swing and at that time everyone was very distracted and not to kin to specifics.

"Don't go home?" He mumbled to himself. It sounded female? Who would say this? Who'd want to bother me with this type of call?" Maybe, a prank call? He continued thinking throughout the day as lunch pasted by and then the afternoon proceeded to arrive. He was finally ending his day and today, due to the extra early celebrations and awards he had a few things to wrap-up and left the office later than normal.

When approaching his street he saw many people walking urgently and in a precipitous manner. He soon approached his home it was in flames, engulfed in fire and by the looks of it the fire had vanquished the whole house.

Samuel was petrified as he looked surprise at his house from about a house or two away, as the firemen, squad cars and emergency vehicles made their way to the house in hopes of saving what ever was left of it. At this point they most surely wanted to contain the fire from spreading to surrounding houses.

"Are you Samuel Ponce?" asked a man in a suit and microphone, he was the local News Organization. "We had reports you were inside? Can you tell us how this happen?" No, Samuel answered as he shrugged away from the cameras and reporters.

Richard Petra his neighbor who was giving an account of how the house exploded into fire and no one knew how or what exactly had happen. Many answers lead to gas explosion, electrical fire, and even chemicals. Jose another neighbor ran over to Samuel he was a quiet neighbor and pulled him aside. Samuel do you have an idea what happen? You know as a veteran I've seen things like this but, they rained in from above. They were dropped from airplanes, or military style helicopters. Do you have any idea? Samuel at this point remembered the call. "Don't go home today" Samuel knew then there was something very clandestine.

Samuel, continued his neighbor to explain that only a bomb could do this type of damage. As he continued to rattle off like all veterans do when reminiscing old war stories, Samuels's thoughts were somewhere else.

Samuel the following morning woke-up at his office. His head was throbbing after sleeping into a stupor that previous night. The guard must've let him in and let him sleep it off in his office. Getting it all together took him several minutes. Why? Why would anyone do this to me? Samuel paced around his office trying to bring together his thoughts, ideas and suspicions. He just couldn't find anything.

After an hour on his office sofa and a coffee prepared by his secretary with a little emulsified whisky to bring him back from his bad dream; Samuel immediately started reviewing the Armed Forces Services Bill for the position he had applied for. He gallantly called Josh; as always Josh wasn't in and he left him a message about what had happened. He was able to talk to his lady friend but, she was sure she did not know anything and had to leave for an important meeting.

Samuel called several of his friends, colleagues and asked for their assistance in investigating what had just happen. They all agreed to help him and soon Samuel was receiving e-mails and faxes from many electronic message centers referring him to the first place he had called; Josh and the Armed Forces Services Program.

One of the most disclosing information was that about the peninsular region where his family had their twenty acres and the recent "imminent domain" paperwork relating to the taking of land by the Government. Also there was the killing of his Grandmother's and how the Department would deal with the press and defend their position. But with these disclosures, there were even more questions like; Why the burning of my house? Was it a bomb? Why the sudden refusal of hiring me to the AFS Committee?

Surprise, Samuel received so much information from his friends he was up to his neck in information to go through. Someway he would have to find from all of these documents the why's, to his questions. It reminded him of how he pieced together the Computer Programming Sequencing that had catapulted him to stardom in the Princeton Campus and his successful profession today.

Since he had no other place to stay Samuel buried himself in his office that first night to continue his search. He was surprised to find minor personal details as; the purchase contract to their first barn his grand parents constructed in the early twenties. Paid tax receipts, house schematics and land surveys, etc. etc. Paperwork that he found were very private and papers that was very old. He continued to place them all in order and saw a particular one that was a Memorandum relating to the "imminent domain" justification written by a Junior Political Steward, dated 1990. That's strange that's exactly the year I started in Princeton!

As he continued reading he was surprised at the potshots taken at his Grandparents and the arrogance to the responses given by them justifying this Officers complaints submitted. The report ended, "for the protection of the United States and the Commonwealth the imminent domain clause supersedes the ruling from the complainant, feeble-minded owners...." It continued and continued, with every word demoralizing, demonizing and suppressing any of his grand parent's petitions and not alone their Constitutional Rights.

As he was finalizing this particular Memorandum the signer was omitted. Reason: "for national security reasons". I guess grand ma's dishing out was kind of strong! What a bunch of cowards! Now that a true reason, the great and mighty needed protection! The poor and victimized, do not?!

Samuel became even more determined to find out whom or whom or what party was really behind this and maybe he can find out more about himself and what had happen to his house. "If I would have arrived just fifteen minutes earlier that night I would have been toast!" he thought as he continued finding out more about his grandparents' acreage and death.

It was about three in the morning when he read into a very important "Confidential"

Report it was the setting up of the new position he applied for several years ago. The position was to create firewalls to outside public access to public Web-sites during inquiries by certain individuals that wanted specific information and had on-going investigations by the Government relating to military entitlements, benefits and awards.

"Now who would drum up this gambit to well deserving citizens and mostly when they apparently needed this important information? Have they heard of the Freedom of Speech?" questioned Samuel, as he continued in disgust of the plan, position and the mission of that created position. In a way he was glad he did not start with that position and God knows he would have not lasted under that iron-fisted dictatorial management.

Samuel nodded off once, twice and soon was awoken by his secretary.

"Here, Samuel I made you some coffee it's eight and soon everyone will be here", she said in a hurry. "You might want to freshen up in Derek's Office".

Samuel woke up surrounded in papers he had reviewed the previous day and night. As he stood up several flew off him and fell to the floor. He looked around to an endless stack of papers he would need to continue investigating. He moved slowly towards the fax machine and focused on a strange paper with the words boldly in red "Secret". "It ain't secret if it's on my desk", Samuel said to himself as he picked it up and started to read it.

It was signed by the candidate selected by the AFS Committee for that position he had applied for. It had every job the individual had had and to Samuels knowledge, they were insignificant and incongruent to what he was interviewed for and was drilled that interview session for. But the surprising part was the approval stamp on the bottom portion of the application. It had Josh Ashcrupt's name and signature.

"Hell To Chamber!" shouted Samuel in Disbelief! What is this? I can't believe it! Samuel kept reading further and more concentrated as ever before!

He put down the grouping of papers and picked-up another. He went back and forth as an accountant that meticulously checks balances on a spreadsheet. Now and again he would review something perplexed, sigh and look at it again, as to corroborate that the distilled spirits of the previous night were not playing a trick on him.

I can't believe this; Grandma was posted for Income Tax Violations! I can't believe this! Who'd want to do this to an old person?! His outburst brought several of his companions into his office; they'd never seen Samuel in such an uproar before. All of them were surprised and baffled by Samuels clamors and spite.

So now its clear Grand Ma and Grand Pa devoted their lives to this country and they get the shaft when they mostly needed it the most! Samuels's head fell lower between his shoulders as he wept over the whole picture that was unfolding before him and conjuring in his mind.

They first bought it legally and straightforward but so that the Armed Forces Services could have their new Computer Training Simulations Center, they needed it close to the missile-firing range and that meant that any properties surrounding the base would need to be purchased; at any cost. They made an offer, made a more stupider offer, harassed them, killed a couple of people, claimed "imminent domain" clause and then killed Grand Ma to conceal the past. Now they're after me! But why? Everyone must know it by now!

As Samuel continued through his papers, in came a fax. There were two sheets of new correspondence from today's investigating! Both marked "Secret" and another "Extremely Secret". Samuel chose the Extremely Secret", just to advance to the end of his mind games and get the final punch of approval of self-doubt he wanted to clarify.

It read; ... all personnel would be immune of data transferred in error and caused ill-manner ordinance of dropping of .... Where's the rest?! Where's the rest of the sentence, dropping of.... What! He looked at the date and it was exactly the date the fire in his house! The fire then had to be premeditated!

Samuel opened the "Secret" memo there was an order to have maneuvers re-routed over another range of quadrant to ensue new maneuver requirements. Signed by Josh Ashcrupt - Strategic Armed Forces Officer.

"Beat-cha!" Samuel smiled and hugged the paper; today the computers win over the simulation!

Chapter 6

MIRRORED PIECES

Samuel was about to leave his office and head for the Sheriff's Office, when the door flung open after a few knocks. Who'd want to see him, he thought to himself. There was his lady friend standing in the winding cold evening air of that fall night.

"Can I come in, it's important?!" She said in an alarming way.

Samuel looked outside and around the premises to see if anyone was with her.

"Come in" he replied in disbelief. "Samuel, you know I love you and I wouldn't do anything to hurt you, right?" As she looked at him persistently, as if she needed to say something but it wouldn't come out or what came out of her mouth was twisted to make it seem caring, sympathetic and prolix.

"Yea, I know, like the position that was created by Josh? And you didn't tell me it was him all along who didn't want me to know?!" Samuel responded with relent composure. "Why? Why if you care for me so much?"

She started recounting her childhood fantasy of becoming the first women Officer and how she had done all that was right to become eligible and be promoted to that eloquent position.

She raised her head at Samuel and started towards him, walking slowly, slowly towards him. She ever-so-slightly moved her hand to the rear of her dress where she had a dagger. She continued her rambling, "Josh, became my Manager he insisted that the first thing in his plan for the military success be to cut-off all those that had benefited from pensions, retirements, disabilities and government seniorities. Then by saving the Government millions of dollars he could justify his plan to bring back the military and military livelihood. He insisted your family was one of them and every time you'd speak to him he'd return to the office with even worse predictions of how you were to be finished off. Obviously, you would become heir to their belongings and land, so he focused on you." She was close enough to Samuel to strike him with the dagger, as she continue to talk she moved in slowly as if she had practiced or rehearsed it several times before.

Samuel stopped her as she drew close and grabbed her arms in a clapping manner.

"You don't get it, I loved you! I wanted us to be together! I didn't feel any hate or animosity towards you or Josh! But it's already uncovered and you have no alternative but to surrender and turn yourselves in!"

As Samuel said those words their lips clasp together in a long awaited rush. She dropped the dagger to the floor and as it hit she tensed, as they looked at it on the floor. Samuel then slapped her, as she fell to the ground he muttered the words, "and you don't seem nice enough for me". He turned and left as he slammed the door and headed towards the Sheriff's Office.

When arriving there was already a call that had stated an alarm of sorts. He was rushed into an office where there stood Clarence and Jaime both whom had sent him information through the electronic e-mail of the "Secret" nature. They all stood there over the similar papers Samuel had just been reviewing.

"What's wrong? Why's everyone here?

"Well, Josh it's a very important man, he commands nothing less but the three-fourths of the military intelligence in the United States? How would you like to screw this one up?"

"My name is Samuel Ponce and I am the next victim on Josh Ashcrupt's agenda. I will give all the necessary complaint's and allegations to move this investigation forward and with this proof, I think we have sufficient evidence that my life was in direct threat by his order and plot."

With those words the Sheriff called the FBI and requested a Search Warrant for Josh Ashcrupt's property. As they were on their way out of the building Samuel heard someone calling him, it was Meliza Stark, his lady friend.

"What are you doing here? Do you still want to kill me and be placed in jail for life?!"

"Samuel I'm here to turn myself in, I know now that what I have done is wrong, and I have conspired with Josh's plan instead of standing up to him. I'm sorry." Meliza began to cry as a Deputy took her away for questioning and to hold until further notice.

Chapter 7

MENDED PIECES

As they reached the building where Josh lived it was humungous, spacious and had a very elaborate landscape. His mansion was in a quiet, high-class and solemn street. "Who'd suspect a criminal in this street?" whispered Samuel to himself. The time was already three am in the morning, yet Samuel felt so strung-out and hyper the time meant nothing to him. As they sat in front of Josh's mansion they noticed a small faint window lit in the basement. The Sheriff who had a team of Deputies ready, moved onto the premises to the small window, they looked in and saw no one. They signaled the Sheriff that gave the remaining Deputies the order to knock on the door and if needed they were prepared with a door rammer to bring the door down and move in. As they knocked no one answered and as they moved to ram the door down, they were surprised by the sudden arrival of a helicopter.

Someone from within the helicopter started firing machine gun fire at the Deputies as they scattered to seek shelter from the bullets. Three officers were down from the fire as the remaining two fired back from behind some cypress trees and cemented fence. As the Sheriff and I fell behind the police cruiser seeking life saving shelter. The Sheriff proceeded to return fire, until the helicopter soon shown the piercing light to where they were at and a rain storm of sparks and bullets started pulsating the police cruiser. It shook like a leave on a windy day. Relentless fire that soon stopped when other police arrived and started firing back at the helicopter. During this time one of the deputies had hammer down the front door and was returning from Josh's mansion.

"You're not going to believe this, but there's a small armory in there and enough communications equipment to talk to someone on the moon!" Sighed the Deputy breathless in exhaustion. By now the helicopter had left and they soon ran heading into the mansion for shelter. Samuel was belated by all the material Josh had in the premises, but the most significant of all was the strategic map on the wall with various close-ups of the small peninsula where his Grand Parents had lived and the elaborate mapping of all the Plans, Programs and Projects there were. As he continued to look closely he saw flight trajectories and maneuvers plans, dates, names of project leaders and assigned focus areas to the sequencing of partials of land that were soon to be acquired by the department.

The mapping had areas still not purchased but marked "executive", as if it were exclusive for certain people and the protection of just certain people. Samuel's thoughts went into a tail-spin thinking of what kind of "exclusivity" would merit the killing and fleecing of true Americans honor and duty?

"There it was. There it is!" exclaimed Samuel, as he pinpointed to his house that was leveled by Josh's' plan to kill him. You see this was no accident, here's the proof! Samuel's finger trembled and shook as he pointed from airbase to the address his house once stood. "You see it was purposely planned! Why would you make people immune to ordinance if it weren't that they were using it to cover-up the bomb being dropped that night!" sparked Samuel.

The Deputy called the Sheriff over to a peculiar box that lay next to the main computer. As they opened it, red-lit numbers were ticking off at: 59. That's right, fifty nine seconds! "Everyone out!" yelled the Sheriff, as everyone looked up from what they were doing.

"What wrong?" asked Samuel. "Don't we need this information? Don't we need more information to find Josh?" Samuel pleaded to the people around him, which soon were gone. "Out everyone! Samuel later, for now, get out!" answered a Deputy as he grabbed him by the shirt collar. As everyone fled out of the mansion, Samuel was jogging slightly behind everyone wondering why the sudden evacuation, when an explosion started like a Fourth of July celebration. Small pops, a little noisier, then a stronger boom - then the whole building was engulfing in flames. Josh had fiendishly booby-trapped the evidence or so that no one could retrieve any evidence.

As the debris of ash and burnt partials filled the air, the Sheriff received a radio communiqué. It was from dispatch, where Meliza was being detained. She had told the investigators about Josh's plot and that he had a warehouse just a few miles up the coast. It was where they made the satellite transmissions to change the flight maneuvers that had exploded Samuel's house.

The sheriff knew he needed to get the FBI and most probably all of the Coast Guard; Special tactical at the Armed Forces Base and other units ready for what may be a very dangerous place and a very dangerous situation.

As they arrived at the warehouse, it looked like a war zone; the agents that had arrived before hand had had a shoot out leaving several bodies littered around the premises. For Samuel he hoped it wasn't Josh's body. The warehouse was the Armed Forces Simulations Center, the same place where Josh made the satellite transmittals to change the flight maneuvers that had exploded Samuel's house.

It looks that Josh had used it as his private access to own government center to conduct his own little demented campaign. "I'm sure no taxpayer knows about this little dirty secret." Expressing himself a little louder this time.

Down from the building came a mob of agents and with them Josh. Josh was handcuffed and seemed very distressed by the loss of his firefight and reputation. Samuel looked at him directly into his eyes to see only darkness and blatant return look of smirk-ness and betrayal. Samuel soon realized his blind devotion for his most closest friend and stared him back in disgust and commented, "So this is the friendship you offered me?"

Josh was maniacal and tried to spit on Samuel. Samuel responded with a left fist surprising him to the chin crippling Josh to the floor. "You're really pathetic!" As Samuel turned to join the Sheriff back to his Officers, he inquisitively looked back at Josh. Josh was wrestling with the agents and was attempting to take the firearm from one of the deputies who cleverly pushed him down on the ground and proceeded to cuff his legs and arms together. 'Put a muffle on him too!" shouted Samuel.

It seemed even in the lowest situations Josh never understood he was a criminal; a travesty to society and the lowest friend Samuel had ever seen sink into total abyss. Samuel pieced some past incidences why he would have ended this way, but Josh came from very good family and everyone has a choice, he had made his own. It seemed for sure the saying for his actions was clear and the saying that fit would be: "what you sow - you will reap".

THE END

EPILOGUE

If you enjoyed this novel and would like to read other p.marquez-garcia novels please see the following selections;

Benito's Treasure hunt, 2000

Flight To The Mountain Top, 2001

Cruise ' in, 2001

Costume, 1999

Printed in the United States
by Baker & Taylor Publisher Services